ABT

A Note to Parents and Caregivers:

Read-it! Joke Books are for children who are moving ahead on the amazing road to reading. These fun books support the acquisition and extension of reading skills as well as a love of books.

Published by the same company that produces *Read-it!* Readers, these books introduce the question/answer and dialogue patterns that help children expand their thinking about language structure and book formats.

When sharing joke books with a child, read in short stretches. Pause often to talk about the meaning of the jokes. The question/answer and dialogue formats work well for this purpose and provide an opportunity to talk about the language and meaning of the jokes. Have the child turn the pages and point to the pictures and familiar words. When you read the jokes, have fun creating the voices of characters or emphasizing some important words. Be sure to reread favorite jokes.

There is no right or wrong way to share books with children. Find time to read with your child, and pass on the legacy of literacy.

Adria F. Klein, Ph.D.
Professor Emeritus
California State University
San Bernardino, California

Editor: Jill Kalz
Designer: Joe Anderson
Page Production: Melissa Kes
Creative Director: Keith Griffin
Editorial Director: Carol Jones
The illustrations in this book were created digitally.

Picture Window Books
5115 Excelsior Boulevard
Suite 232
Minneapolis, MN 55416
877-845-8392
www.picturewindowbooks.com

Printed in the United States of America.

Library of Congress Cataloging-in-Publication Data
Donahue, Jill L.
Laughing letters and nutty numerals : a book of jokes about ABCs and 123s /
by Jill L. Donahue ; illustrated by Zachary Trover.
p. cm. — (Read-it! joke books—supercharged!)
Includes bibliographical references.
ISBN-13: 978-1-4048-2365-5 (hardcover)
ISBN-10: 1-4048-2365-4 (hardcover)
1. Alphabet—Juvenile humor. 2. Numerals—Juvenile humor. 3. Riddles, Juvenile.
I. Trover, Zachary. II. Title. III. Series.
PN6231.A45D66 2006
818'.602—dc22   2006003566

Laughing Letters and Nutty Numerals

A Book of Jokes About
ABCs and 123s

by Jill L. Donahue
illustrated by Zachary Trover

Special thanks to our advisers for their expertise:

Adria F. Klein, Ph.D.
Professor Emeritus, California State University
San Bernardino, California

Susan Kesselring, M.A.
Literacy Educator
Rosemount–Apple Valley–Eagan (Minnesota) School District

PICTURE WINDOW BOOKS
Minneapolis, Minnesota

What is the difference between a new penny and an old quarter?

Twenty-four cents.

Son: "Dad, can you help me find the common denominator in this problem?"

Dad: "Don't tell me they haven't found that yet. They were looking for that when I was a kid."

What is the longest word in the English language?

Smiles, *because there is a mile between the first and last letters.*

Where can you buy a ruler that is 3 feet long?
At a yard sale.

What is the difference between here and there?
The letter T.

Which letters are the smartest?
The Ys.

What did one math book say to the other math book?
"Man, have I got problems!"

What kind of ant can count?
An accountant.

Why does Lucy like the letter K?
Because it makes Lucy lucky.

What is the coldest letter?
C, because it is in the middle of ice.

Why is the letter T like an island?
It is in the middle of water.

How many peas are there in a pint?
There is only one P in pint.

How do you spell *cold* with only two letters?

IC.

How do you spell *we* with two letters, but without using the letters W and E?

U and I.

Why is it dangerous to do math in the jungle?

If you add four and four, you get "ate."

How do you spell *too much* with two letters?
XS.

Why is the letter A like a flower?
Because a B comes after it.

Why is the number 9 like a peacock?
Because without its tail, it is nothing.

What kind of pliers do you use in math class?
Multipliers.

What word becomes smaller when you add two letters to it?
Small.

How many letters are there in the alphabet?
Eleven: T-H-E-A-L-P-H-A-B-E-T.

How are 2+2=5 and your left hand alike?
Neither is right.

The alphabet goes from A to Z. What goes from Z to A?
A zebra.

How much dirt is there in a hole that is 1 foot deep and 1 foot across?

None. A hole is empty.

Why is the letter B hot?

Because it makes oil boil.

How many feet are in a yard?
It depends how many people are standing in it.

What is in the middle of March?
The letter R.

What increases in value when you turn it upside down?
The number 6.

When you take away two letters from this five-letter word, you get one. What word is it?
Stone.

How can you spell *eighty* in only two letters?
AT.

From what number can you take away half and be left with nothing?

The number 8. If you take away the top half, you have "o" left.

What is the center of gravity?

The letter V.

Which two letters of the alphabet are nothing?
MT.

When do mathematicians die?
When their numbers are up.

Which three letters of the alphabet frighten all criminals?
FBI.

What letter should you avoid?

The letter A, because it makes men mean.

What eight-letter word has one letter in it?

Envelope.

What letter can make you very wet?
  The C.

What two words have thousands of letters in them?
  Post office.

What five-letter word has six left when you take two letters away?
  Sixty.

VA NISH

How can you make varnish disappear?
Take out the R.

What did the zero say to the eight?
"Nice belt."

What is abcdefghijklmnopqrstuvwxyz, slurp?
Someone eating alphabet soup.

What do math teachers eat?

Square meals.

If all of the letters of the alphabet were invited to a tea party, which letters would be late?

U, V, W, X, Y, and Z, because they all come after T.

Why shouldn't you put the letter M in the freezer?

Because it turns ice to mice.

How can you say *rabbit* without using the letter R?
Bunny.

Why is six afraid of seven?
Because seven ate nine.

What kind of table has no legs?
  A multiplication table.

Which word in the dictionary is spelled incorrectly?
  Incorrectly.

What kind of tree is a math teacher's favorite?
  Geometry.

Read-it! Joke Books— Supercharged!

Chitchat Chuckles: A Book of Funny Talk 1-4048-1160-5

Creepy Crawlers: A Book of Bug Jokes 1-4048-0627-X

Fur, Feathers, and Fun! A Book of Animal Jokes 1-4048-1161-3

Lunchbox Laughs: A Book of Food Jokes 1-4048-0963-5

Mind Knots: A Book of Riddles 1-4048-1162-1

Nutty Names: A Book of Name Jokes 1-4048-1163-X

Roaring with Laughter: A Book of Animal Jokes 1-4048-0628-8

Sit! Stay! Laugh! A Book of Pet Jokes 1-4048-0629-6

Wacky Workers: A Book of Job Jokes 1-4048-1164-8

What's Up, Doc? A Book of Doctor Jokes 1-4048-1165-6

Artful Antics: A Book of Art, Music, and Theater Jokes
    1-4048-2363-8

Family Follies: A Book of Family Jokes 1-4048-2362-X

What's in a Name? A Book of Name Jokes 1-4048-2364-6

Looking for a specific title or level? A complete list
of *Read-it!* Readers is available on our Web site:
www.picturewindowbooks.com